Mr. Gator Hits the Beach

By Julie McLaughlin
Illustration by Ann Marie McKay

LEGACY PUBLICATIONS

For my precious granddaughter, Marley Rose McLaughlin.
Julie McLaughlin

For my grandchildren and all the children I have visited in the
Head Start program and in the elementary schools.
Ann Marie McKay

———————

As I reflect upon the success of the "Gator books," I would be remiss in not thanking
God first for his blessings and encouragement to follow my dream. Special thanks to my junior
editors and fellow belly surfers Jake, Walker and Balen Williams; Lydia and William Smith; and
Marianna Murray. Thanks to all of the educators, parents and children who continue to support
the Gator books around the state and beyond. Thanks so much to Legacy Publications for their
expert staff and ability to create a beautiful finished product. Thanks to my typist extraordinaire,
Julie Thould, for her excellent skills and patience. Special thanks to my gifted and talented
friend, Judy Reese, for creating the map for *Mr. Gator Hits the Beach*. Thanks to the many
professionals at South Carolina Department of Natural Resources, especially Lynda Creek, for
sharing their knowledge of coastal wildlife. Last but not least I would like to thank my
illustrator and friend, Ann Marie McKay, for sharing this wonderful experience with me.
Julie McLaughlin

Text © 2008 Julie McLaughlin / Illustration © Ann Marie McKay
The illustrations were done in watercolor.

Library of Congress Control Number: 2008936977
ISBN: 978-0-933101-56-2
Library of Congress Summary: Mr. Gator's summer vacation is interrupted when
he takes a detour to the Atlantic Ocean with Lilly, the loggerhead turtle.

Legacy Publications, 1301 Carolina Street, Greensboro, NC 27401 / www.Legacypublications.com
Printed in Canada by Friesens

One of the nicest things about living in the South
Carolina Lowcountry is having easy access to our beautiful
barrier islands and beaches on the Atlantic Ocean. People come
from all over every summer to enjoy sunny beach vacations.

Freshwater ponds and estuaries are often nestled nearby, and
are home to numerous alligators as well as other wildlife.
Although it is rare, sometimes alligators end up on the beach
or in the ocean. After consulting with quite a few experts,
I found that the main reasons are these:

• droughts drive the gators to other bodies of water,
• saltwater baths can rid them of parasites,
• gators can roam around during mating season, or
• the destruction of habitat sends them traveling.

Finding an alligator in the ocean does not happen often, but
when it does, response is quick, and the gator is soon removed
and relocated back to its natural habitat.

We hope you have enjoyed the Gator book series —
Hungry Mr. Gator, Mr. Gator's Up the Creek, and finally,
Mr. Gator Hits the Beach. It has been a pleasure sharing the
South Carolina Lowcountry wetlands, its coastal regions,
and the fauna and flora that inhabit them.

Julie McLaughlin   Ann Marie McKay

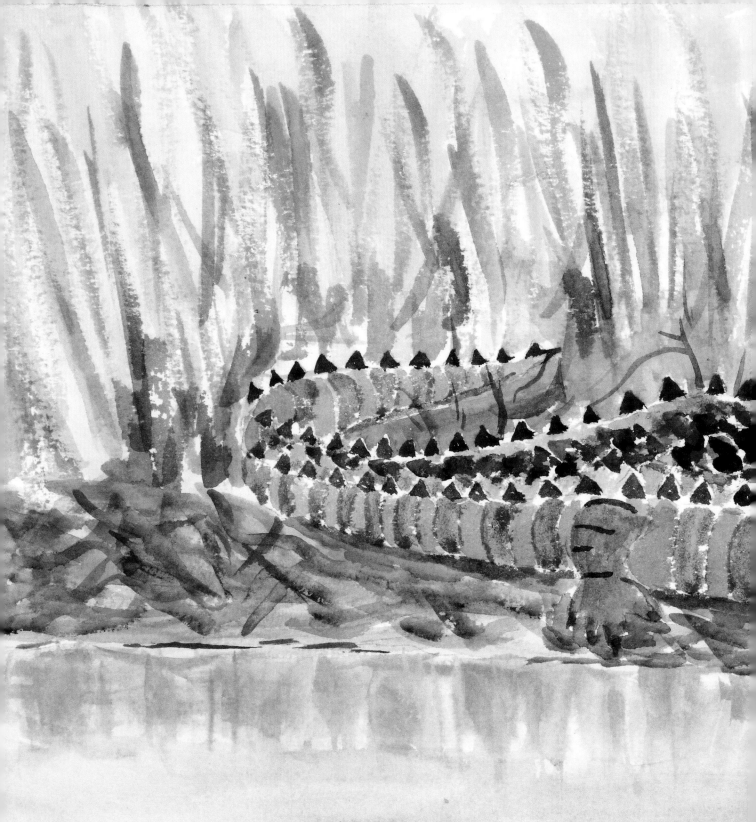

Mr. Gator stretched out on the bank and stared down at his sad reflection shimmering in the water below.

"Ho-hum," he sighed. "There's nothing to do around here. I'm tired of the same old this and the same old that!"

Just at that moment, a wood stork flew overhead. "Special delivery!" he croaked. Mr. Gator looked up and noticed a piece of paper fluttering down from the sky like a feather from a bird.

It landed smack in the middle of Mr. Gator's snout. He stared at the paper and saw that it was a letter from his old friend, Big Al.

July 1

Dear Mr. Gator,

I hope you are well. I'm heading south for a gator family reunion and a little vacation. Why don't you take a vacation yourself and come stay at my place while I'm gone? The scenery at Bull Island is beautiful, and the fishing is great!

No need to reply, the place is always open.

Your gator pal,
Big Al

"A vacation," thought Mr. Gator, growing more excited by the minute. "Why, that's exactly what I need." He decided to leave right away. He swam up the creek toward his vacation and away from boredom.

When Mr. Gator reached the Cooper River, he swam under the tall Ravenel Bridge, on past the South Carolina Aquarium and the gray **USS** *Yorktown* aircraft carrier. He stayed close to the shore, away from the channel, so the big ships and other boats wouldn't run over him in the harbor.

Intracoastal Waterway

Soon he turned left, leaving the harbor, and headed toward the Intracoastal Waterway.

Mr. Gator saw all kinds of sights on his journey—children crabbing
and throwing a cast net for shrimp from a floating dock, and a family of
ospreys perched in their nest high atop a pole. The parents were busily
pushing fresh-caught pieces of fish into their chicks' open, hungry beaks.
A sailboat glided through the waterway with ease, as the summer breeze
gently filled its sails.

Mr. Gator dove under the water to cool off from the hot summer sun. A strange-looking creature swam gracefully in front of him. Trying to be friendly, Mr. Gator swam closer to introduce himself. "Hello," he said. "I'm an alligator. My name is Mr. Gator, and I'm on vacation!"

"Hello, yourself," replied the strange creature. "I'm Lilly, a loggerhead sea turtle, and I've come a very long way to lay more than 100 eggs high up on the beach in the sand."

"Wow!" said Mr. Gator, very impressed. Forgetting all about Big Al's place, he asked, "May I watch?"

"I think not!" exclaimed Lilly. "And besides, I won't be laying my eggs until later tonight. Then I'll find the perfect sandy spot in the dunes to dig my nest. But we can swim together in the ocean for a while if you like."

"The ocean?" said Mr. Gator. "I've never been to the ocean."

"Then follow me, Mr. Gator," said Lilly, as she took a sharp turn into the inlet toward the Atlantic Ocean.

Mr. Gator swam as fast as he could to keep up with his speedy new friend. The water soon became saltier and stung Mr. Gator's eyes.

Lilly and Mr. Gator swam to the surface for a look and found themselves facing the shore. They saw children building sandcastles and collecting seashells with their families on the beach. Sandpipers hurried along the shore, searching for bits of shellfish and insects washed up by the tide.

Some of the boys and girls were in the ocean, lying on boards facing the beach. They waited patiently for the perfect breaking wave to send them racing toward the shore.

"That looks like fun!" exclaimed Mr. Gator. "I guess so," said Lilly. "It's called surfing. I see it all the time."

"I think I'll give it a try!" said Mr. Gator, very excited.
He pointed his snout toward the beach and caught a huge wave.
"Yippee!" he yelled. "Look at me! I'm belly surfing!"
"Come back, Mr. Gator," shouted Lilly. "There's trouble that way!"
But Mr. Gator couldn't hear her over the roar of the waves.

People on the beach watched as this fearsome creature came riding a wave toward the shore. Folks ran from the water yelling, "It's a sea monster!" "No, it's a shark!" "Look out, it's a GATOR!"

SPLAT! Mr. Gator crashed onto the beach with mighty force, exploding a sandcastle in every direction.

Mr. Gator shook the grains of sand from his snout. Out of nowhere, he noticed two men in uniforms running down the beach toward him with ropes and long nets in their hands. "Don't worry, folks," the two men shouted. "We'll capture that misplaced reptile!"

Just before the men reached him, Mr. Gator turned back into the ocean. He was so frightened that he was afraid to look back. Under the ocean he swam, far, far away from the shore, but he didn't have any idea where he was going.

Lilly, the sea turtle, quickly came to his rescue. "This way, Mr. Gator!" she cried in a hurried voice. "Follow me!"

Mr. Gator didn't have any trouble keeping up with Lilly this time. She led him safely back to the waterway and calmer waters.

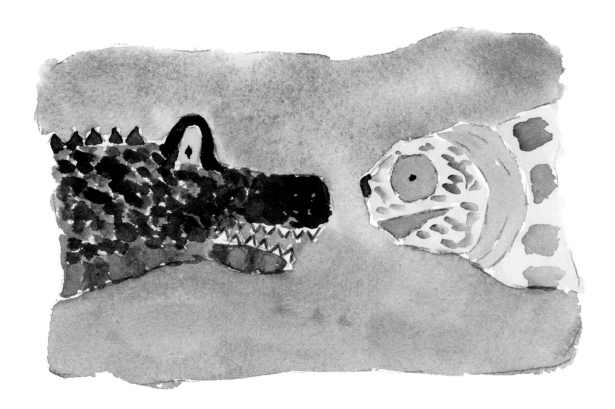

Even though he was out of breath, Mr. Gator managed to thank Lilly for saving him.

"Think nothing of it, Mr. Gator. You're my friend, and friends help each other. Now that you're safe, I guess you're anxious to go on with your vacation."

"Oh, I've had quite enough vacation," said Mr. Gator in a tired voice. "But thanks to you, I have a lot of memories of my day at the beach."

"You certainly do," said Lilly. "The ocean is my home, but somehow I don't think it's the place for you."

"I think you're right, Lilly," said Mr. Gator, "and speaking of home, that's just where I'm going. Good luck with your eggs, Lilly."

"Good luck to you, too," said Lilly.

When they had finished their goodbyes, the two friends parted, going their separate ways.

Later that night, the full Carolina moon lit the way for
Lilly's long, slow trek to the shore . . .

. . . and found tired Mr. Gator curled up in his cozy bed sleeping—
as much as an alligator can.

Two months later . . .

Amazing alligator facts

1. There are two species of alligators: the American alligator and the Chinese alligator. The American alligator can grow up to 19 feet long, weighing up to 600 pounds. The Chinese alligator grows to about 6 feet long.

2. Alligators have five toes per foot in front, and four toes in back.

3. Alligators use their powerful tails to move very quickly in the water, but they move more slowly on land. However, they can lunge and run suddenly for short distances.

4. Alligators are very valuable to their wetland habitats because they dig gator holes. They use their mouths and claws to dig out an area that will hold water during dry seasons for themselves and to share with other animals, fish, and insects.

5. Alligators eat almost anything, including fish, birds, and mammals. Alligators swallow their prey whole.

6. Alligators have no vocal cords, but during mating season, males can make a loud, bellowing roar to warn off other males by sucking air into their lungs and blowing it out.

7. Alligators sleep intermittently throughout the day and occasionally at night. They are nocturnal by nature. They never enter a deep, dreamlike sleep like humans. Alligators are wired to wake up at the slightest disturbance. This is clearly an important trait for survival.

Mr. Gator's glossary

Aircraft carrier: A warship with a flight deck on which airplanes can take off and land.

American alligator: A large reptile with very sharp teeth, powerful jaws, and a shorter, broader snout than a crocodile.

Atlantic Ocean: The ocean bordering the East Coast of the United States. It is one of five oceans of salt water connecting to cover 70 percent of the Earth's surface.

Bull Island: A barrier island of great natural beauty along the South Carolina coast between Georgetown and Charleston. It is home to extensive wetlands and wildlife and is part of the Cape Romain National Wildlife Refuge.

Cast net: A net thrown into the water to catch fish or shrimp.

Channel: The deeper part of a river or harbor.

Floating dock: A floating platform, anchored near a shoreline, that rises and falls with the tide.

Harbor: A part of a body of water protected and deep enough for a ship to anchor.

Inlet: A narrow water passage between nearby islands.

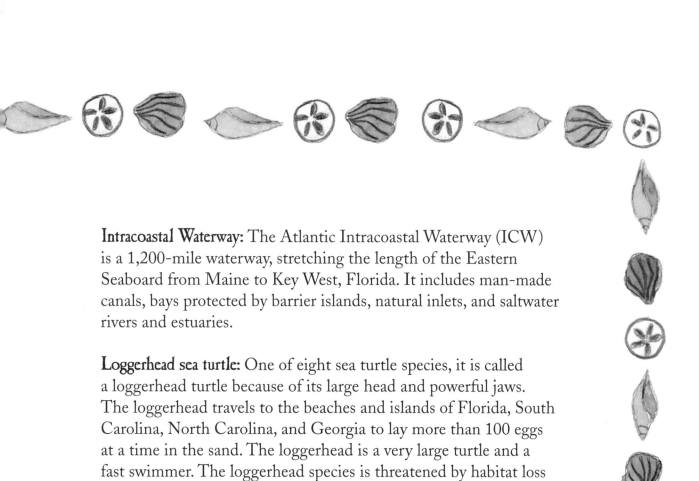

Intracoastal Waterway: The Atlantic Intracoastal Waterway (ICW) is a 1,200-mile waterway, stretching the length of the Eastern Seaboard from Maine to Key West, Florida. It includes man-made canals, bays protected by barrier islands, natural inlets, and saltwater rivers and estuaries.

Loggerhead sea turtle: One of eight sea turtle species, it is called a loggerhead turtle because of its large head and powerful jaws. The loggerhead travels to the beaches and islands of Florida, South Carolina, North Carolina, and Georgia to lay more than 100 eggs at a time in the sand. The loggerhead is a very large turtle and a fast swimmer. The loggerhead species is threatened by habitat loss and because they drown in shrimp trawls. The loggerhead is South Carolina's State Reptile.

Osprey: A large, long-winged fish hawk living in habitats near rivers, lakes, and seacoasts. An osprey's nest is made up of a bulky mass of sticks and debris, usually built in treetops or atop telephone poles. Some are built on rocks or flat ground.

Sandpiper: A small shorebird with a long, soft-tipped bill. These birds live on the seashore in all parts of the world. They follow the shoreline looking for bits of food. There are 89 species of sandpipers.

Wood stork: Formerly known as a wood ibis, the wood stork is the only true stork native to the United States. It lives near the coast, chiefly in cypress swamps. Its neck and head are bald. Its naked gray head earned the stork the nickname of "flinthead."

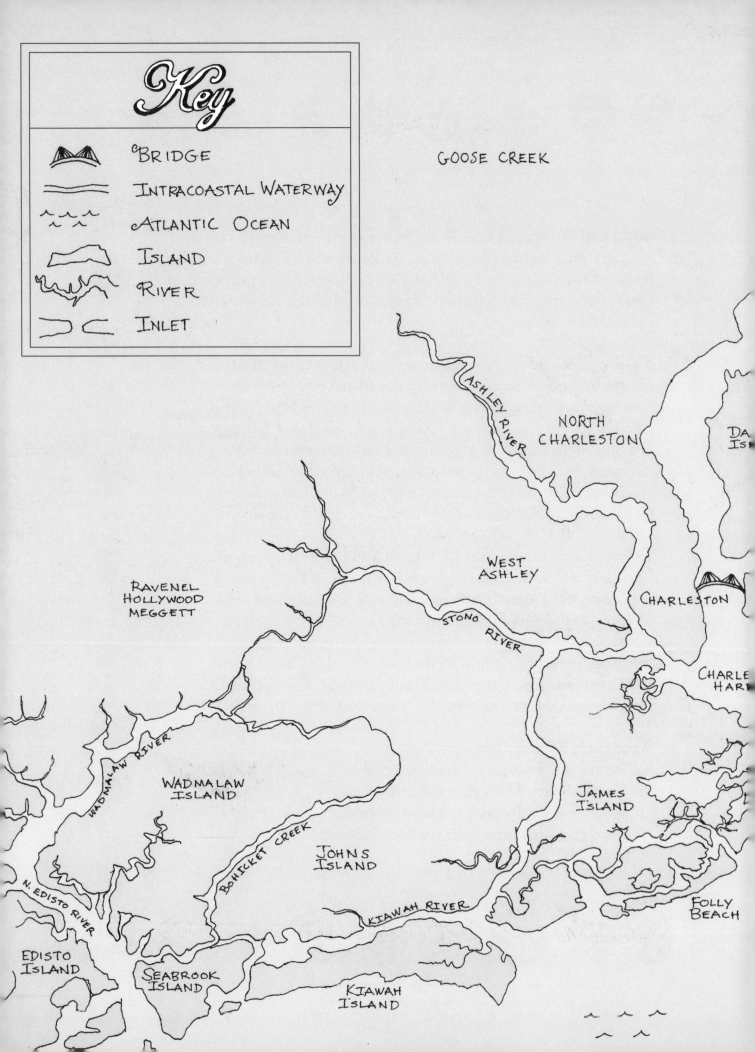

Key

🌉 Bridge

〰 Intracoastal Waterway

～～ Atlantic Ocean

⌒ Island

River

)(Inlet

GOOSE CREEK

ASHLEY RIVER

NORTH CHARLESTON

DA IS...

WEST ASHLEY

CHARLESTON

RAVENEL
HOLLYWOOD
MEGGETT

STONO RIVER

CHARLE...
HAR...

WADMALAW RIVER

WADMALAW ISLAND

JAMES ISLAND

BOHICKET CREEK

JOHNS ISLAND

N. EDISTO RIVER

KIAWAH RIVER

FOLLY BEACH

EDISTO ISLAND

SEABROOK ISLAND

KIAWAH ISLAND